I0451413

WEDDED BLISS
A PARANORMAL HOLIDAY ROMANCE

NORTH POLE UNIVERSITY
BOOK SIX

MARIE-HELENE LEBEAULT

CONTENTS

PROLOGUE: THE QUESTION

CONNOR

The meteorite felt like a frozen star in my pocket.

I'd carried it for three weeks, since the night after our record-breaking flight when Magnus pulled me aside in the Sacred Grounds and pressed the raw chunk of space metal into my palm. "For when you're ready," he'd said, aurora light reflecting in his knowing gaze. "Nix helped me enchant it. The metal remembers crossing between worlds. Seemed fitting."

Now, standing outside Crystal Dining Hall with graduation chaos swirling around us and Kayla's hand warm in mine, the ring I'd forged from that meteorite burned against my thigh like a promise I was finally brave enough to make.

"Connor?" Kayla squeezed my fingers, her green eyes searching my face. "You've been quiet since the ceremony ended. Are you okay?"

Around us, graduates streamed past in clusters, sprites launching into aerial acrobatics, elves conjuring champagne fountains, reindeer shifters racing toward the Sacred Grounds for the traditional post-graduation bonding run. The whole campus hummed with celebration and bittersweet goodbyes, but all I could focus on was the woman beside me and the question lodged in my throat.

"I'm perfect," I managed. "Just thinking."

"Dangerous habit." She bumped her shoulder against mine, teasing, but I caught the flicker of concern in her expression. We'd been through too much this year, my family's shattered reputation, her brutal Oath Keeper trials, the Council's scrutiny, proving that human-shifter bonds could work, for her not to recognize when I was holding something back.

I needed to do this right. Needed the moment to match what she meant to me.

"Walk with me?" I tugged her away from the dining hall's entrance, toward the path that wound through the Frosted Gardens. "There's something I want to show you."

"Show me, or tell me?" She fell into step beside me, her graduation gown whispering against the snow-packed ground. "Because you're doing that thing where you get all intense and brooding, and honestly, Prancer, after the year we've had..."

"Trust me." I brought her hand to my lips, kissed her knuckles. "Please?"

Her expression softened. "Always."

The Frosted Gardens were quieter, most students having migrated toward the louder celebrations near the dorms or the Sacred Grounds. Ice sculptures lined the pathways, conjured by this year's advanced Cryomancy class, depicting scenes from North Pole University's history. We passed a rendering of the first sleigh team, another of Santa signing the Creature Accords, a third showing the founding of the Oath Keeper program.

I led Kayla to the heart of the gardens, where an ancient evergreen stretched toward the perpetual twilight sky, its branches heavy with enchanted icicles that chimed softly in the arctic breeze. The aurora borealis danced overhead, ribbons of green and gold weaving patterns that seemed to pulse in time with my racing heart.

"This tree," I said, stopping beneath its canopy, "was planted the year the university opened. Five hundred years ago."

Kayla tilted her head back, studying the glittering branches. "It's beautiful."

"Every Headmaster has added one enchantment to it. Protection spells, mostly. Preservation magic." I turned to face her fully, capturing both her hands in mine. "But also blessings. For students who gather here. For promises made in its shadow."

Understanding flickered across her face. Her breath caught. "Connor..."

"Let me say this." My voice came out rougher than intended. "Before I lose my nerve."

She nodded, squeezing my hands so tightly I felt her pulse hammering against my palms.

"Four years ago," I began, "I walked onto this campus convinced I knew exactly who I was supposed to be. Prancer's heir. Future lead reindeer. Legacy defender." I huffed a laugh. "Turns out I didn't know anything."

"You knew how to be insufferable," Kayla offered, her lips quirking despite the tears gathering in her eyes. "You had that down perfectly."

"I did." I brushed my thumb across her cheekbone, catching a stray tear before it could fall. "And you knew how to call me on it. From that first day in Intro to Sleigh Dynamics when you corrected my form and I wanted to be furious but mostly just wanted to know everything about the human girl who wasn't afraid of a shifter twice her size."

"You weren't that intimidating." Her voice wavered. "Your antlers were still a little crooked from summer molt."

"They were rugged," I protested. "Character-building."

She laughed, the sound breaking through her tears. "Sure. We'll call it that."

"Kayla. Love." I squeezed her hands, grounding us both. "Let me finish before we both fall apart."

She bit her lip, nodded again.

"You taught me that legacy isn't about blood or reputation. It's about choice." I released one of her hands to reach into my pocket, my fingers closing around the ring. "You showed me that strength means building bridges, not walls. That loving you, being loved by you, doesn't make me less of a shifter. It makes me more of who I'm meant to be."

The aurora flared above us, as if the North Pole itself was holding its breath.

"We've proven everyone wrong," I continued. "Every doubt, every whisper that humans and shifters couldn't really bond, that the magic wouldn't hold, that we were too different, we shattered all of it. Together."

"Together," Kayla echoed, her free hand moving to rest over her heart, where I knew she could feel the phantom warmth of our connection even without a formal bond seal.

I dropped to one knee.

Her sharp inhale cut through the night air. Behind us, I heard footsteps pause on the garden path, other students noticing, stopping to watch, but I kept my focus locked on Kayla's face.

I wished Dad could see this. But maybe, somehow, he did.

"I don't have speeches," I said, pulling the ring free and holding it up between us. Starlight caught in the meteorite metal, making it gleam like captured aurora. "Just this truth: You are my home, Kayla Matthews. My partner. The person I want beside me for every flight, every challenge, every impossible dream we decide to chase. You make me braver. Better. You make me believe in magic I can't see but feel every time you look at me like I hung the moon."

A laugh bubbled out of her, half-sob, half-joy. "You didn't hang it. That's not scientifically..."

"Kayla." I smiled up at her. "Will you marry me? Will you let me spend the rest of my life proving that choosing you was the easiest and best decision I ever made?"

For a heartbeat, the world held its breath.

Then she was pulling me to my feet, her hands framing my face, her yes tumbling out between kisses pressed to my lips, my cheeks, the corner of my jaw.

"Yes," she gasped. "Yes, you impossible reindeer. Yes, always yes."

My hands shook as I slid the ring onto her finger. The meteorite band fit perfectly, of course it did, I'd measured her finger while she slept, sneaking the string away before she woke, and the moment the metal touched her skin, it pulsed with soft golden light, then softened, the light dimming until it shimmered faintly beneath her skin, like a promise etched in gold.

"It's warm," Kayla breathed, staring at the glowing ring.

"Magnus and Nix enchanted it. The metal crossed between worlds before it reached Earth, just like we're bridging two worlds." I threaded my fingers through hers, watching the faint shimmer play beneath the surface. "It'll always lead you home. To me."

"I'm already home," she whispered, and kissed me again.

Applause erupted around us.

I'd forgotten about the gathering crowd, graduates who'd followed us into the gardens, drawn by whatever magic hung thick in the air. But when I looked up, my throat tightened.

Magnus and Nix stood at the front, Magnus's arm around Nix's shoulder, both of them grinning. Rowan and Ivy were there too, Ivy actually crying happy tears while Rowan tried and failed to look composed. Elian had Fiona tucked against his side, both of them radiating approval.

But it was Oliver, standing slightly apart with his arms crossed and a rare, genuine smile softening his usually stern features, who nodded at me with something that looked like pride.

"About damn time, Prancer," Sally called from somewhere in the crowd. "We were starting to think you'd lost your nerve."

"Never," I called back, pulling Kayla closer. "Just waiting for the perfect moment."

"Under the Blessing Tree at graduation?" Nix's voice carried clearly despite the growing noise. "I'd say you nailed it."

The aurora overhead suddenly blazed brilliant green-gold, brighter than I'd ever seen it, bright enough that several students gasped and pointed. Threads of light spiraled down from the sky, weaving around the ancient evergreen's branches, around Kayla and me, until we stood in a column of pure northern magic, ancient, sentient, approving.

"The North Pole approves," Oliver said dryly, though his eyes gleamed with emotion. "Apparently enthusiastically."

Kayla laughed against my chest, her arms wrapped tight around my waist. "Does it always do that?"

"Only for bonds the land recognizes as true," Magnus answered. He and Nix moved closer, Nix reaching out to admire Kayla's ring. "Congratulations, both of you. Though I have to say, Connor, I was hoping you'd manage to surprise her. Kayla, did you suspect?"

"Not even a little," Kayla admitted, holding up her hand so the meteorite could catch the aurora light. "I thought he was just being weird about the graduation ending."

"I was being romantic," I protested.

"You were being weird," she countered, but the joy in her voice made it clear she didn't care.

More friends pressed in, congratulations and hugs, and excited chatter about wedding plans we hadn't even begun to consider. Someone conjured champagne glasses, though Sally apparently conjured too many because suddenly Elian was juggling three flutes while trying not to spill on Fiona's dress. Ivy immediately started talking venues, and Crystal, who'd appeared from somewhere in the crowd, was already suggesting they hold one ceremony in London and one here.

"Two weddings?" Kayla's eyes went wide.

"One for your family," Crystal said practically. "One for ours. Makes sense, doesn't it?"

Kayla looked at me, and I could see the wheels turning in her mind, already planning, already building bridges between her two worlds.

"We'll figure it out," I promised her quietly.

Through it all, I kept Kayla anchored to my side, her hand in mine, her ring glinting like a promise made solid.

Eventually, the crowd began to disperse, other celebrations calling, the night still young despite the late hour. Magnus pulled me aside for a brief moment while Nix distracted Kayla with talk of dress shopping.

"You did good, kid," Magnus said quietly. "Your father would be proud."

The mention of Dad sent warmth through my chest instead of the old, familiar ache. He'd been gone for five years now, hadn't lived to see me restore the Prancer name or find the love of my life. But somehow, standing here with Magnus, who'd been more mentor and father figure than I'd deserved, the grief felt gentler. Like maybe Dad really had seen this moment, somehow.

"Thanks," I managed. "For everything. The ring, the enchantment, the support..."

"That's what pack does." Magnus squeezed my shoulder. "Now comes the real work, though. The proposal was the easy part."

I glanced at Kayla, watching her laugh at something Ivy said, her whole face lit with happiness. The aurora still danced overhead, softer now but steady, like the land itself was keeping vigil.

"Building a life together," I murmured, echoing the thought that had been circling my mind since I first decided to propose. "Yeah. That's the real magic."

Magnus smiled. "Smart man. You're learning."

As the night deepened and the celebrations finally began to wind down, I found myself alone with Kayla again, the two of us walking slowly back toward the residential halls. Her head rested on my shoulder, my arm wrapped around her waist, and the comfortable silence between us felt like its own kind of promise.

"So," she said eventually, her voice drowsy but content. "How long have you been planning this?"

"Since the flight trials," I admitted. "Maybe before. Hard to pinpoint exactly when I knew."

"Knew what?"

"That I wanted forever with you." I pressed a kiss to her temple. "That anything less wouldn't be enough."

She stopped walking, turning to face me fully. In the aurora's gentle glow, she looked ethereal, my human girl who'd conquered an impossible university, who'd earned the respect of creatures ten times her age, who'd loved me despite every reason not to.

"Forever sounds perfect," she whispered, reaching up to cup my cheek. "Let's start building it tomorrow."

"Tomorrow," I agreed.

But first, I kissed my fiancée under the North Pole sky, tasting her smile and her tears and her laughter, feeling the weight of the ring on her finger and the rightness of this moment settling into my bones.

The proposal was the easy part.

Now came the real magic: building a life.

CHAPTER ONE
TRANSITIONS

KAYLA

The summons came three days after Connor proposed.

I stared at the cream-colored envelope on my dorm room desk, Santa's official seal pressed into crimson wax, and tried to convince myself this was normal. That being called to the administrative wing for a private meeting with Santa Claus himself was just another Tuesday at North Pole University.

"You're spiraling," Crystal observed from her bed, where she was supposedly packing but mostly watching me pace. "I can actually see the anxiety radiating off you."

"I'm not spiraling." I picked up the envelope again, as if the fourth reading would reveal some hidden context I'd missed. "I'm... processing."

"You've been processing for twenty minutes." She swung her legs off the bed, crossing to take the envelope from my hands. "It's probably about graduation honors. Or maybe he wants to congratulate you on the engagement. You did get proposed to under the Blessing Tree with the entire senior class watching."

"And the aurora exploding like magical fireworks," I added, remembering the way the northern lights had blazed so bright that students could see it from the residential halls. "Very subtle."

Crystal grinned. "Connor doesn't do subtle. It's one of his more endearing qualities."

I sank onto my desk chair, fidgeting with my engagement ring. The meteorite metal was cool against my skin now, though sometimes, like when Connor held my hand or when I thought about him, it would warm, and a faint golden shimmer would appear beneath the surface. Magnus's enchantment work was extraordinary.

"What if it's bad news?" I asked quietly. "What if the Council decided that Connor and I passing all our trials wasn't enough, that they want more proof that human-shifter bonds can work?"

"Then you show them more proof." Crystal's voice went fierce. "Kayla, you survived the Oath Keeper trials. You broke records. You earned Oliver's respect, which is basically like getting a glacier to smile. If anyone questions your place here..."

A knock interrupted her passionate defense.

Connor pushed through the door without waiting for an answer, his presence filling the small dorm room with the scent of winter wind and pine. He'd been out flying, his hair was windswept, his cheeks flushed from the cold, and his eyes held that bright contentment he always had after time in the sky.

"Hey." He crossed to me immediately, bending to press a kiss to my temple. "Got your message. What's wrong?"

I held up Santa's envelope.

His eyebrows rose. "Ah. When?"

"Tomorrow morning. Ten o'clock." I leaned into his solid warmth, letting his calm anchor my spinning thoughts. "You?"

"Got mine an hour ago." He pulled a matching envelope from his jacket pocket. "Same time. Looks like we're both summoned."

Crystal made a thoughtful sound. "Together? That's either really good or really bad."

"Thanks for that analysis," I muttered.

Connor's hand found the back of my neck, his thumb rubbing soothing circles against my skin. "It's probably about next steps. Career placement, maybe. The university likes to meet with graduating seniors about their post-NPU plans."

"Most graduating seniors aren't engaged to reindeer shifters who just broke five-hundred-year-old flight records," I pointed out.

"True." His lips quirked. "But most graduating seniors also didn't become the first human Oath Keeper in university history. We're kind of a package deal of unprecedented circumstances."

Despite my anxiety, I smiled. "Is that what we're calling it?"

"I'm open to suggestions." He tugged me to my feet, wrapping his arms around my waist. "How about 'legendary power couple'? 'Barrier-breaking duo'? 'The reason Oliver started drinking his whiskey earlier in the day?'"

I laughed against his chest. "That last one is probably accurate."

Crystal cleared her throat meaningfully. "I'm going to give you two some privacy. Also because watching you be adorable reminds me I need to get back to London soon. I have a case briefing Monday morning."

"Thanks for coming up to help," Connor called as she grabbed her jacket.

"Wouldn't miss it," Crystal shot back with a grin. "Besides, someone had to make sure you didn't talk Kayla into eloping and skipping the actual weddings. Your family would never forgive you."

The door clicked shut behind her, leaving Connor and me alone in the rapidly dimming afternoon light. Through the window, I could see snow beginning to fall, the gentle, magical kind that NPU conjured when the weather felt too still.

"Talk to me," Connor murmured, his chin resting on top of my head. "What's really worrying you?"

I was quiet for a moment, gathering my thoughts. Connor never pushed, one of the things I loved about him. He simply waited, patient and solid, until I was ready to voice the fears tangling in my chest.

"What if he keeps you here and sends me back to London?" I finally whispered. "What if building a life together means choosing between love and purpose?"

His arms tightened around me. "Then we figure it out. Together."

"That's not an answer."

"It's the only answer that matters." He pulled back enough to cup my face, forcing me to meet his steady gaze. "Kayla, I didn't propose to you under the Blessing Tree so we could spend the next fifty years on opposite sides of the world. Whatever Santa offers tomorrow, whatever the Council wants, we face it as partners. We negotiate. We compromise. We build bridges."

"That's my line," I said, but the knot in my chest loosened slightly.

"I'm learning from the best." He kissed my forehead, then my nose, then finally my lips, soft and sweet and full of promise. "Besides, have you considered that maybe they want to offer us something together? Something that uses both our skills?"

"Like what?"

"I don't know. But we've spent four years proving that humans and shifters can work together, learn together, succeed together. Maybe they want to build on that."

It was a nice thought. Hopeful. Very Connor.

I wanted to believe it.

THE NEXT MORNING dawned clear and cold, the kind of arctic brilliance that made everything look carved from crystal and starlight. Connor met me outside the administrative wing, looking unfairly handsome in dark pants and a forest-green sweater that made his eyes seem even more vivid.

"Ready?" he asked, offering his hand.

I took it, feeling the now-familiar warmth spread from his palm to mine. "As I'll ever be."

The administrative wing was quieter than the academic buildings, with thicker carpets, older wood, and portraits of previous Headmasters watching from gilded frames. A sprite secretary smiled at us from behind an ornate desk, gesturing toward the double doors at the hall's end.

"He's expecting you. Go right in."

The office beyond was exactly as I remembered from my first visit to NPU, floor-to-ceiling windows overlooking the campus, shelves crammed with books and magical artifacts, a desk that looked like it had been carved from a single piece of ancient oak. But instead of just Santa sitting behind that desk, Sally Dancer stood beside him, along with a stern-looking elf woman I recognized as Council Elder Frost.

"Kayla, Connor." Santa's warm voice filled the room as he gestured to the chairs opposite his desk. "Thank you for coming. Please, sit."

We settled into the offered chairs, Connor's hand finding mine automatically.

"First," Santa continued, his blue eyes twinkling, "congratulations on your engagement. The aurora's response was quite enthusiastic. The North Pole clearly approves of your bond."

"Thank you, sir," Connor said.

"Second, congratulations on your respective achievements this year. Kayla, your performance in the Oath Keeper trials was extraordinary. Connor, that flight record will stand in university history." Santa leaned forward, folding his hands on the desk. "Which brings us to why you're here."

My heart hammered against my ribs.

"The Council and I have been discussing the future of magical education," Santa said. "North Pole University has served us well for five centuries, but the world is changing. More humans are discovering magic. More creatures are integrating with human society. The barriers between our worlds are thinning."

Elder Frost spoke for the first time, her voice crisp. "We need institutions that reflect this reality, ones where difference isn't tolerated, it's foundational. Programs that train not just creatures in magic, but humans and creatures in cooperation."

"We're building a new academy," Magnus added, stepping forward with barely contained excitement. "North Pole Academy, a secondary school for younger students, ages eleven to eighteen. A place where human children with magical sensitivity can learn alongside young creatures. Where integration starts early, before prejudices take root."

My breath caught. Connor's hand tightened on mine.

"We want you to lead it," Santa said simply, looking at Connor. "Headmaster Prancer has a certain ring to it, don't you think?"

Connor went very still beside me. "Sir, I..."

"And Kayla." Santa's gaze shifted to me. "We'd like you to serve as Director of Human-Creature Relations, with a seat on the Academy's governing board. Your experience navigating both worlds makes you uniquely qualified to help shape curriculum and policy."

"This is unprecedented," Elder Frost said, though her tone

suggested approval rather than concern. "Building an academy from the ground up. Creating new educational models. It will require vision, dedication, and the kind of bridge-building you two have demonstrated throughout your time here."

I couldn't speak. Couldn't process. Beside me, Connor seemed equally stunned.

"You don't have to answer now," Magnus said gently. "This is a big decision. But the Council believes, I believe, that you two are exactly what this academy needs. What the future needs."

"When?" Connor managed. "When would this... start?"

"Construction begins this summer," Santa replied. "We're hoping to open next fall for our first class of students. Which means you'd have approximately a year to build curriculum, hire staff, and establish protocols." He smiled. "I hear you're planning a wedding. Perhaps good timing to launch both a marriage and a career?"

Connor looked at me. I looked at him.

In his eyes, I saw the same mixture of terror and exhilaration that was probably reflected in my own.

"Can we think about it?" I asked, finding my voice.

"Of course." Santa stood, signaling the end of the meeting. "Take a few days. Discuss it together. But know this, the Council chose you not despite your youth or your unprecedented bond, but because of it. You represent the future we're trying to build."

As we left the office in a daze, Magnus caught my elbow. "Hey. Breathe."

I realized I'd been holding my breath since Santa said "Headmaster Prancer."

"This is insane," Connor said, running a hand through his hair. "They want us to build a school. An entire school."

"They want you to build bridges," Magnus corrected. "Which

is what you've been doing since the day you met. Just... on a larger scale."

"What if we fail?" The question escaped before I could stop it.

Magnus's expression softened. "Then you fail together. But Kayla? You won't. I've watched you two accomplish impossible things for four years. This is just the next impossible thing."

Connor and I walked back across campus in silence, hands clasped, minds racing. Students passed us in clusters, laughing and shouting, blissfully unaware that their futures, and ours, had just shifted on their axis.

"What are you thinking?" Connor finally asked as we reached the Frosted Gardens.

I stopped walking, turning to face him fully. Snow drifted around us, soft and quiet, and the Blessing Tree's branches chimed their gentle song.

"I'm thinking," I said slowly, "that a year ago, I couldn't have imagined this. Any of this. You, us, the life we're building."

"Is that a good thing?"

"It's terrifying." I stepped closer, resting my hands on his chest. "And exciting. And exactly right."

His eyes searched mine. "Are you saying..."

"I'm saying yes." The words came easier than I expected. "Let's build a school, Connor. Let's build a future where what we have and what we have proven is possible becomes the norm. Expected. Celebrated."

"Together?" His voice held wonder.

"Always together." I rose on my toes, kissing him softly. "Besides, someone needs to make sure Headmaster Prancer doesn't let the power go to his head."

He laughed, the sound bright and free, pulling me close. "Director Matthews has a nice ring to it too."

"Are we really doing this?"

"We're really doing this."

The girl who'd held Santa's envelope with shaking hands yesterday wouldn't have believed this. But today, she was saying yes to everything.

Above us, the aurora began to dance, subtle, approving, ancient magic welcoming the next impossible dream.

We'd start with a wedding. Two of them, actually, one in London for my family, one here for our magical community. We'd celebrate our bond in both worlds, honoring every part of who we were.

CHAPTER TWO
THE DRESS & DOUBTS

KAYLA

The London boutique smelled like roses and old magic.

I stood in the middle of the elegant shop, surrounded by mirrors and cream-colored wallpaper, while Crystal flipped through a rack of white dresses with the focus of someone on a military operation. My mother sat on a velvet settee near the window, sipping tea and trying not to cry every time she looked at me.

"This is surreal," I muttered, watching Crystal pull out dress after dress. "Three weeks ago, I was taking finals. Now I'm shopping for a wedding dress."

"Two wedding dresses," Crystal corrected, holding up a sleek column gown that looked like it belonged on a runway. "Don't forget the bonding ceremony. Though I suppose the dress for that one will be... different."

"Enchanted," I said quietly. "The elf consultant said it would transform during the ritual. Show the bond marks forming. Respond to the aurora."

Mom's teacup rattled slightly against its saucer. She still wasn't entirely comfortable with the magical aspects of my life, the fact that I was marrying a reindeer shifter, that I'd survived trials designed to break humans, that I could see and touch magic most people didn't even know existed.

But she was trying. That counted for something.

"Let's focus on the London dress first," Crystal said diplomatically. "The one your family will see. The traditional one."

"Right." I took the column gown from her hands, studying the clean lines and delicate beading. "Traditional."

Except nothing about my life was traditional anymore.

An hour later, I'd tried on twelve dresses and rejected them all.

Too fussy. Too plain. Too much like I was playing dress-up in someone else's fantasy. Too formal for a girl who'd spent four years wearing enchanted snow gear and studying magical theory.

Dress thirteen had a sweetheart neckline and enough tulle to make me look like a cupcake. I wanted to cry.

"Kayla?" Crystal's voice came through the curtain. "You okay in there?"

"I hate this one too," I admitted, my voice thick.

"Then take it off. We'll find another."

"What if we don't?" The fear spilled out before I could stop it. "What if I can't find a dress because I don't actually belong in this world either? The human world, I mean. What if I'm too magical for London and too human for the North Pole and I'm just... stuck between?"

Silence.

Then the curtain swept aside and Crystal stepped into the dressing room, ignoring the shop attendant's protest about privacy. She took one look at my face and pulled me into a fierce hug, tulle and all.

"You're spiraling again," she said gently.

"I'm allowed to spiral. I'm getting married in six weeks and starting a job building a school from scratch, and I don't even know if I can find a dress that feels like me."

Crystal pulled back, gripping my shoulders. "The dress is just fabric. Yes, you want to feel beautiful. Yes, you want Connor to see you walking down the aisle and forget how to breathe. But Kayla? You could wear jeans and a t-shirt and he'd still look at you like you hung the moon."

"The stars," I corrected automatically. "He said I hung the stars."

"See? You even remember his terrible romantic metaphors." She smiled. "That's love. The dress is just decoration."

I wiped my eyes, smudging what little makeup I'd bothered with. "I don't feel like I belong anywhere right now. Not fully human anymore, not magical enough to be anything else. Just... between."

"Good," Crystal said firmly. "Between is exactly where you need to be. You're a bridge, remember? Bridges don't belong to either side, they connect them."

The curtain rustled again, and my mother appeared, her expression gentle but determined. "May I?"

Crystal squeezed my hand and slipped out, leaving Mom and me alone in the small space.

"I know this is hard," Mom said softly. "I know your life has changed in ways I can barely understand. Magic and shifters and universities at the North Pole, it's like something out of a storybook."

"But real," I whispered.

"But real," she agreed. She reached out, adjusting a piece of tulle that had gone crooked. "And I know you're worried about fitting in. About being enough for both worlds. But sweetheart, you've always been between things. Between cautious and brave. Between practical and dreamers. Between your father's logic and my faith."

I blinked at her, surprised.

"Being between doesn't mean you don't belong," Mom continued. "It means you belong to something bigger. Something that needs both sides to exist." She smiled, tears shining in her eyes. "You're marrying a man who loves every complicated, contradictory part of you. The human part and the magical part and everything in between. Don't you think he'd want you to wear a dress that honors all of it?"

Something loosened in my chest.

"I don't know what that dress looks like," I admitted.

"Then let's find it." Mom pushed the curtain open, gesturing me back out into the main shop. "But first, get out of that cupcake. It's not doing you any favors."

I laughed, the sound watery but genuine.

Twenty minutes and three more dresses later, the shop owner emerged from the back room carrying a gown I hadn't seen before. It was wrapped in silvery tissue paper, and when she laid it across a chair, something about it made my breath catch.

"This just arrived," she said, her accent placing her somewhere in Eastern Europe. "Custom order for another client, but she canceled. I think perhaps it was meant for you instead."

Crystal raised an eyebrow. "That's very mystical of you."

The shop owner smiled. "I've been fitting brides for forty years. Sometimes the dress chooses the girl."

I approached slowly, reaching out to touch the fabric. Silk, cool and smooth beneath my fingers. But as I lifted it, I noticed subtle shimmer woven through the material, not quite white, not quite silver, like captured moonlight.

"It has enchantments," I breathed.

The shop owner's smile deepened. "Light ones. Preservation spells, mostly. To keep the dress perfect through the ceremony. But also..." She gestured to the bodice. "Try it on. You'll see."

In the dressing room, with Crystal's help, I slipped into the gown.

It fit like it had been made for me. The bodice hugged my curves without being too tight; the neckline was elegant but not revealing. The skirt flowed in soft layers that moved like water. But it was the details that made me fall in love, tiny crystal beading that caught the light, a subtle train that didn't drag, and sleeves that were sheer enough to show skin but structured enough to feel substantial.

"Oh," Crystal whispered when I emerged. "Kayla."

Mom pressed her hand to her mouth, tears spilling over.

I turned to the mirror and froze. Elegant enough for a London church. Enchanted enough for the North Pole. Not too human. Not too magical. Just... me.

"This is the one," I said, my voice barely above a whisper.

The shop owner appeared at my elbow, approval in her knowing eyes. "It will transform, you know. During your bonding ceremony."

I met her gaze in the mirror. "How did you..."

"I told you. Forty years of fitting brides." She reached out, adjusting the sleeve slightly. "This dress has magic woven into its very threads. In your human ceremony, it will look exactly as it does now. But when you speak your vows at the North Pole, under the aurora, the enchantments will wake. The shimmer will become visible. The crystal beading will glow. It will show the world, both worlds, the bond you're creating."

Crystal made a small sound of delight. "That's perfect."

The shop owner's expression grew thoughtful. "Few seamstresses know how to weave this kind of enchantment anymore. Old magic. Forgotten by most."

Something in her tone made me pause. "Why forgotten?"

"Times change. Traditions fade." She smoothed an invisible wrinkle from the skirt. "But some bonds deserve the old rituals. The old recognition."

The London ceremony was for my family, I realized. The bonding ritual would be for the magic.

"It's expensive," Mom said practically, though her eyes were still wet.

"It's perfect," I repeated, and I meant it.

The shop owner quoted a price that made Mom wince, but before anyone could protest, Crystal pulled out a credit card. "Wedding gift from Magnus and me. No arguments."

"Crystal..."

"No arguments," she said firmly. "You're my best friend and you're marrying into the Prancer pack. Let me do this."

I hugged her, careful not to wrinkle the dress, feeling grateful and overwhelmed and exactly right all at once.

As the shop owner carefully wrapped the gown and made arrangements for alterations, I caught my reflection in the mirror again. In the perfect dress, surrounded by the people I loved, I didn't look like someone stuck between worlds.

I looked like someone who'd found exactly where she belonged.

"One dress down," Crystal said cheerfully as we left the shop, the precious garment bag slung over her arm. "Now we just have to plan two weddings, build a school, and get you married before fall term starts."

"Is that all?" I asked dryly.

Mom linked her arm through mine. "You've survived worse."

I thought about the countless moments of doubt and fear and determination.

"Yeah," I said, smiling. "I have."

The London streets bustled around us, tourists and locals, the normal human world going about its normal human day. But I carried a dress enchanted with North Pole magic, engaged to a reindeer shifter, planning a life that spanned both worlds.

CHAPTER THREE
PASSING THE TORCH

CONNOR

The Sacred Grounds had never felt more sacred than they did tonight.

I stood at the edge of the clearing, watching the last rays of twilight paint the snow in shades of purple and gold. The aurora was already beginning to dance overhead, gentle tonight, respectful of the ceremony about to take place. Around me, the pack gathered in silence. Magnus and Nix. Rowan. Elian. Oliver standing slightly apart, as always, but present. And Sally, the young reindeer shifter who would inherit what I was about to give up.

The lead harness hung from an ancient post at the clearing's center, gleaming with centuries of use and magic. My father had worn it. My grandfather. Every Prancer lead reindeer stretching back to the original twelve who'd pulled Santa's first sleigh.

Tonight, I would be the last.

"You ready for this?" Sally appeared at my elbow, her expression determined and focused, so different from the nervous first-year I'd mentored three years ago. "Last chance to back out and stay on the team."

"I'm ready." And I was. The decision had settled into my bones with surprising ease once Kayla and I accepted Santa's offer. I couldn't be Headmaster of the new academy and lead reindeer. Something had to give, and this, this I could pass on knowing it was going to someone worthy.

"Good." Sally's eyes gleamed with barely contained excitement. "Because I've been working toward this since freshman year, and if you changed your mind now, I might actually cry."

"No crying at ceremonial harness transfers," I said with mock seriousness.

"Fine. But I'd be very disappointed." Her grin was infectious. "In a dignified, lead-reindeer-appropriate way."

Oliver's voice cut through the gathering darkness. "It's time."

The pack formed a circle around the central post, and I walked forward alone. This was my moment, my choice, and tradition dictated I face it without support. Even Kayla waited at the circle's edge, her green eyes reflecting aurora light, her engagement ring catching the glow.

I reached the post and lifted the harness with both hands. The leather was warm despite the cold, thrumming with generations of magic and purpose. For a heartbeat, I could feel every Prancer who'd worn it, their strength, their pride, their dedication to the flight.

"Connor Prancer," Oliver said, stepping into the circle. "You were born to this harness. Why do you choose to lay it down?"

The ritual question. One I'd been preparing to answer for weeks.

"Because legacy isn't just what we inherit," I said clearly, my voice steady. "It's what we choose to build. My father taught me to honor tradition. Magnus taught me that tradition evolves. And

Kayla..." I found her in the circle, held her gaze. "Kayla taught me that the greatest legacy isn't the one we're born into. It's the one we create for those who come after."

Oliver nodded once. "And who do you choose to carry this forward?"

"Sally Dancer." I turned to face her. "Step forward." Sally moved into the circle, her usual brightness replaced by something deeper. Reverence. Understanding of what this moment meant. I held out the harness.

"You came to NPU three years ago nervous and uncertain, convinced you weren't fast enough or strong enough to make the team. But you worked harder than anyone I've ever trained. You understand that being lead isn't about individual glory. It's about the team. The pack. The mission." My throat tightened.

"You'll carry this harness with honor, and I'm proud to pass it to you." Sally took the harness with trembling hands. For a moment, we stood there, mentor and student, two reindeer shifters bound by pack and the weight of history.

"I won't let you down," she said quietly, her voice steady despite the emotion in her eyes. "Or your father's memory."

"I know." I gripped her shoulder. "Take care of them. They're yours now, but someday, they'll be the ones teaching the next rookies." Her eyes gleamed with understanding.

"The circle continues."

She stepped back, and Oliver moved forward with an ancient ring, silver and etched with runes I couldn't quite read. "Kneel."

I dropped to one knee in the snow.

"Connor Prancer, the pack releases you from your oath to the sleigh team. You are no longer bound by harness and flight, but by choice and purpose." Oliver placed the ring in my palm. It was warm, almost hot, and I felt magic pulse through the metal. "This ring belonged to the first Headmaster of North Pole University.

Santa asks that you wear it as you build the academy. As a reminder that some legacies are meant to be shared, not hoarded."

I slipped the ring onto my right hand. It fit perfectly, and the moment it settled against my skin, I felt something shift. The harness's magic, which had hummed in my blood for four years, quieted. Not gone, I'd always be a reindeer shifter, always carry my father's legacy, but transformed into something new.

"Rise, Headmaster Prancer," Oliver said.

I stood, and the pack erupted into howls and cheers. Sally immediately pulled me into a crushing hug, the harness caught between us.

"Speech," someone called, probably Elian. "The retiring lead owes us a speech!"

I laughed, stepping back from Sally. "You want a speech? Fine." I looked around the circle, at the shifters who'd become my pack, my family. "Four years ago, I thought I knew exactly who I was supposed to be. Prancer's heir. Future lead. Defender of a legacy I barely understood."

The aurora brightened overhead, as if listening.

"Then I met a human girl who challenged everything I thought I knew about strength and magic and what it meant to build something lasting." I found Kayla again, saw tears on her cheeks, and love in her eyes. "She taught me that the best legacies aren't the ones we preserve in amber. They're the ones we let grow and change and become something better than what we inherited."

Magnus was nodding, Nix pressed against his side.

"So yeah, I'm laying down the lead harness. But I'm not walking away from who I am or where I come from. I'm taking everything my father taught me, everything this pack taught me, and I'm building something new. Something that honors the past by making space for the future." I grinned at Sally. "Besides, you all get Sally as lead now. She's going to be extraordinary."

More laughter, more cheers. The sacred formality of the ceremony dissolved into celebration, pack members pressing forward with congratulations and teasing remarks about my new administrative duties.

But it was Santa who appeared at my elbow as the crowd began to disperse toward the warming fires someone had conjured at the clearing's edge.

"Walk with me," he said quietly.

We moved away from the celebration, toward the tree line where the aurora's light painted the snow in shifting colors.

"That was well done," Santa said. "The pack respects your choice."

"Thank you, sir."

"The Council will watch the academy closely, you know." His tone was gentle but serious. "What you and Kayla are building, it's unprecedented. There will be resistance. Questions."

I nodded, having expected this. "We can handle it."

"I believe you can." Santa stopped walking, turning to face me fully. "But Connor, you need to understand something. This academy isn't just about education. It's about proving that integration can work not just at the university level, but earlier when beliefs and prejudices are still forming. When young minds are most open to change."

"I know."

"The Council isn't united on this. Elder Frost supports you, as do Magnus and several others. But some believe the old ways should remain old. That humans and creatures should stay separate, that mixing the two will dilute magical bloodlines or compromise our security." His blue eyes were sharp despite their kindness. "They're watching for you to fail."

A chill that had nothing to do with the arctic cold ran down my spine. "Are you saying..."

"I'm saying be careful. Be thorough. Build your academy on such solid ground that even your critics can't deny its success." Santa placed a hand on my shoulder. "And Connor? Trust your instincts. Both yours and Kayla's. You're not just Headmaster. You're partners building something together. That's your greatest strength."

Before I could respond, Kayla appeared through the trees, wrapped in her winter coat and looking concerned. "Sorry to interrupt. Crystal said you wanted me?"

Santa smiled. "I did. I wanted to give you both something." He reached into his coat and pulled out an ornate key, old brass, etched with the same runes as the ring on my finger. "This is the key to the academy site. Tomorrow, if you'd like, I can show you the land where you'll build your future."

Kayla took the key reverently, and I moved to her side, wrapping an arm around her waist.

"Thank you," she whispered.

"Thank you both," Santa corrected. "For taking this leap. For believing in a dream that isn't fully formed yet. For being brave enough to build bridges others are afraid to cross."

He left us there at the forest's edge, and Kayla leaned into me, the key warm in her gloved hand.

"How are you feeling?" she asked. "About the harness?"

I thought about it, really thought about the loss and the gain, the ending and the beginning. "Lighter than I expected. Ready."

She held up the key so it caught the aurora light. "We're really doing this."

"We really are."

From the clearing behind us came sounds of celebration, Sally probably showing off with the harness already, the pack toasting to new beginnings and honored traditions. My bachelor party would come later, sometime in the next few weeks before the London wedding. Tonight was just about this, the passing of one dream to make room for another.

"Do you think they'll accept us?" Kayla asked quietly. "The students. Their families. The magical community."

"Some will. Some won't." I turned her to face me, cupping her cheek with my free hand. "But we're not building the academy for everyone. We're building it for the kids who need it. The ones who don't fit the old categories. The ones who'll change the world if someone just gives them the chance."

She smiled. "When did you get so wise?"

"I'm learning from the best." I kissed her softly, tasting snow and hope and the future we were choosing together. "Come on. Let's get back to the celebration. Sally is probably already planning elaborate flight patterns she'll never actually pull off."

"And Nix is definitely planning my bachelorette party without asking me first."

We walked back toward the fires hand in hand, the key to our future tucked safely in Kayla's pocket. The aurora blazed brighter behind us, ancient magic acknowledging the shift, approving the choice.

I no longer carried the harness, but somehow, I felt more grounded than ever.

Some legacies were meant to be carried. Others were meant to be transformed.

CHAPTER FOUR
THE LONDON WEDDING

KAYLA

The morning of my wedding dawned grey and drizzly, typical London weather that somehow felt perfect.

I stood at the window of the bridal suite, watching rain streak down the glass, and tried to calm the butterflies rioting in my stomach. Behind me, Crystal wrestled with the zipper on her bridesmaid dress while my mother fussed with flower arrangements that didn't need fussing.

"You're being very quiet," Crystal observed, finally getting the zipper to cooperate. "Should I be worried?"

"No." I turned from the window, managing a smile. "Just... processing."

"You've been processing a lot lately." She crossed to me, taking my hands. "Cold feet? Because if you need to run, I have the getaway car keys and a solid alibi prepared."

I laughed despite my nerves. "Not cold feet. Just big feelings."

Mom appeared with my dress, the enchanted gown we'd found in that magical boutique. In the soft morning light, the shimmer in the fabric was barely visible, waiting for the bonding ceremony to fully wake. But I could feel the magic humming beneath the silk, patient and alive.

"Let's get you into this," Mom said gently. "Your father's already downstairs pacing holes in the carpet, and we're due at the church in an hour."

The dress slid over my head like water, settling against my skin with the weight of dreams and promises. Crystal fastened the buttons while Mom adjusted the train, and when I finally turned to the mirror, my breath caught.

I looked like a bride. Not the uncertain girl who'd arrived at North Pole University four years ago, not the human struggling to prove herself in a magical world, just a woman about to marry the love of her life.

"Oh, sweetheart," Mom whispered, tears already forming. "You're beautiful."

A knock at the door interrupted the moment. Dad poked his head in, then froze when he saw me.

"Can I come in?" His voice was gruff with emotion. "Or is it bad luck?"

"Come in, Dad." I held out my hand, and he crossed to me, looking distinguished in his formal suit and slightly uncomfortable with the boutonniere Mom had insisted on.

"You look just like your mother did," he said quietly. "On our wedding day. Beautiful and brave and absolutely terrifying."

"Terrifying?"

"Marriage is terrifying." He smiled. "In the best possible way. You're choosing to build a life with someone, to trust them with your worst days and your best dreams. That takes courage."

"Connor's worth the courage," I said simply.

"I know." Dad pulled a small box from his pocket. "Your mother and I wanted to give you something. It's tradition, something old, something new, something borrowed, something blue."

Inside the box was a delicate bracelet, silver filigree with tiny sapphires woven through. "It was your grandmother's," Mom explained. "She wore it on her wedding day, and I wore it on mine."

Crystal helped me fasten it around my wrist, and I felt the weight of generations settling alongside the enchanted dress. Old magic and new, human tradition and supernatural promise, all braided together.

"Thank you," I whispered, hugging them both.

The church was small but beautiful, grey stone covered in ivy, stained glass windows casting colored light across wooden pews. My extended family filled the seats, along with a handful of friends from before NPU. But scattered among them were the magical guests, Crystal and Magnus, Nix wearing a glamour that made her look fully human, Rowan and Ivy, Elian and Fiona. Oliver had declined, citing discomfort with human ceremonies, but he'd sent a gift: an ancient blessing carved in Old Norse.

I waited in the vestibule with Dad, listening to the string quartet play soft prelude music. Through the crack in the door, I could see Connor at the altar with Elian beside him as best man; family standing with family.

"He's nervous," Dad observed. "That's good. Means he knows how lucky he is."

The music shifted, marking the beginning of the processional. Crystal squeezed my hand once and slipped through the door, gliding down the aisle in her soft blue dress. Then it was just Dad and me, and the beginning of everything.

"Ready?" he asked.

I thought about the last four years. The trials. The growth. The love that had bloomed between Connor and me despite every reason it shouldn't work. The future we were building, one impossible bridge at a time.

"I'm ready."

The doors opened, and every face turned toward me. But I only saw Connor.

His expression when he caught sight of me - wonder and love, and something that looked like relief - made my heart soar. I watched his hands unclench, watched him take a shaky breath, watched his eyes shine with tears he was too proud to let fall in front of everyone.

Dad walked me down the aisle slowly, and I tried to memorize everything. The way the light streamed through the stained glass. The smell of roses and old stone. The faces of people I loved witnessing this moment. But mostly, I memorized Connor, the way he looked at me like I was magic itself.

When we reached the altar, Dad placed my hand in Connor's. "Take care of her," he said quietly.

"With my life," Connor promised.

The vicar began the ceremony, traditional words about love and commitment, about building a life together and weathering whatever storms might come. But I barely heard him. All my focus was on Connor's hand in mine, his thumb drawing circles on my palm, the warmth of him beside me.

"The couple has prepared their own vows," the vicar announced.

Connor went first, his voice steady despite the emotion in his eyes. "Kayla, four years ago, you walked into my life and challenged everything I thought I knew. You were supposed to be just another student, human, temporary, someone who'd pass through NPU and disappear. But you became my partner. My best friend. The person who taught me that strength isn't about power or legacy, it's about choosing love even when it's hard."

His grip tightened on my hands. "You've proven that bridges can be built across any divide if both sides are willing to reach. You've shown me that being vulnerable isn't weakness, it's the bravest thing we can do. And you've made me believe in a future I never imagined possible."

Outside, the rain intensified, but inside, soft light made everything glow.

"I promise to be your partner in all things," Connor continued. "To build bridges alongside you. To catch you when you fall and cheer you on when you soar." He smiled, a little watery. "I promise to love you with everything I am, in this world and the next, for all the days we're given."

My turn. I took a shaky breath, willing my voice not to break.

"Connor, when I came to North Pole University, I was terrified. Terrified of failing, of not being enough. But you saw me, really saw me, and never once asked me to be anything other than myself."

Tears were streaming down my face now, but I didn't care. "You challenged me to be braver. To reach further. To believe I could belong in spaces that weren't designed for me. And you loved me through every doubt, every fear, every moment I wanted to give up."

Through the open church door, I heard a rumble of thunder, or maybe it was something else. Something magical responding to the vows being spoken.

"I promise to be your home," I said. "Your safe place. The person who believes in you even when you doubt yourself. I promise to build the impossible with you, bridges no one thought could stand. Schools and dreams and a life that honors where we come from while reaching for where we're going." I smiled through my tears. "I promise to always love you as you are. My best friend and my heart. Forever."

The vicar's voice seemed to come from far away. "By the power vested in me, I now pronounce you husband and wife. You may kiss the bride."

Connor pulled me close, and the kiss was everything, tender and passionate and full of promise. Around us, the guests erupted in applause, but in that moment, it was just us. Just Connor and me and the life we were beginning.

When we finally broke apart, I noticed something strange. The rain outside had stopped, and through the stained glass windows, impossibly, northern lights danced across the grey London sky.

"Did you..." I started.

"Not me," Connor whispered, his eyes wide. "The North Pole. It's celebrating with us."

Crystal caught my eye from the front pew and grinned, pointing subtly upward. The other magical guests looked delighted, this kind of phenomenon was rare outside the arctic, a sign that the land itself approved of the bond being formed.

We walked back down the aisle hand in hand, husband and wife, while the aurora blazed overhead and our families cheered.

The reception hall was small, strung with fairy lights and filled with laughter. It was exactly what we wanted.

Dad gave a speech about watching me grow from a curious child into a confident woman. He managed only to tear up twice, and he carefully avoided mentioning magic or shifters, though I saw him catch Connor's eye at one point and nod with clear approval.

Crystal's speech was funnier, full of stories from NPU that she carefully edited for human ears. "When Kayla first arrived at university," she said, her eyes twinkling, "she was convinced she wouldn't fit in. But she did more than fit, she excelled. She became the kind of student, the kind of person, that others looked up to.

And watching her fall in love with Connor has been the greatest privilege of my life."

She raised her glass. "To Kayla and Connor. May your love always be as strong as it is today, and may you never stop building bridges."

"To Kayla and Connor!" the guests echoed.

Elian's best man speech was perfect, warm and funny without crossing any lines, talking about growing up with Connor, watching him restore the Prancer name, and knowing that Kayla was exactly the partner his cousin deserved. My more conservative relatives approved, and Connor's eyes were suspiciously bright by the end.

Then it was time for our first dance.

Connor led me onto the floor as the opening notes of our song began, something soft and romantic that we'd chosen together during a late-night planning session. His hand settled at my waist, mine on his shoulder, and we began to move.

"Hello, Mrs. Prancer," he murmured, his breath warm against my ear.

"Hello, Mr. Prancer." I leaned into him, letting the music and his presence wash over me. "We did it."

"First one down." He pulled back enough to meet my eyes. "Ready for the second?"

The bonding ceremony. The magical ritual that would seal our bond in a way the human ceremony couldn't. The transformation of my dress from elegant to enchanted, the appearance of the bond marks, the witnessing by the North Pole itself.

"Ready," I promised.

We danced through the song, and then others joined us. My parents swayed together in a corner, Magnus spinning Nix with practiced ease, Crystal somehow charming one of the older professors into a dance despite his initial protests about "not having moved like this in a century."

The aurora still danced outside, visible through the hall's windows, a reminder that magic was real and watching and celebrating alongside us.

As the evening wore on and the party grew louder, Connor and I slipped outside for a moment of quiet. The air was cool and clean after the rain, and the northern lights painted everything in shades of green and gold.

"Thank you," I said softly. "For giving me this. The human ceremony. The chance for my family to be part of our beginning."

"They're my family too now," Connor reminded me. He wrapped his arms around me from behind, his chin resting on my shoulder. "And next week, your family becomes mine officially. In front of the pack, under the aurora, with all the magic we've been holding back."

I turned in his arms, looping my hands behind my neck. "It's going to be different."

"It's going to be perfect." He kissed me softly. "Both ceremonies. Both parts of who we are. That's what makes us work."

Inside, someone called for us to cut the cake. Outside, the aurora blazed brighter, as if in agreement.

CHAPTER FIVE
CROSSING BETWEEN WORLDS

CONNOR

The portal shimmered in the London hotel room like a tear in reality itself.

I stood with Kayla in front of it, our hands clasped, our formal wedding clothes exchanged for enchanted winter gear that would protect us from the arctic cold on the other side. Through the rippling surface, I could see hints of the North Pole, aurora light, snow, and the familiar landscape of home.

"Ready?" I asked, squeezing her hand.

Kayla looked beautiful in her snow gear, her hair braided back, her green eyes bright with anticipation and nerves. We'd spent three days in London after the wedding, giving her family time to celebrate before we crossed back to the magical world for the bonding ceremony.

"I'm ready." She rose on her toes to kiss me quickly. "Let's go home."

We stepped through together.

The transition was instant, London's grey skies replaced by

winter's bite, city sounds giving way to the whisper of snow and wind. We emerged in the portal chamber beneath North Pole University, where Magnus waited with a grin and open arms.

"Welcome back, Mr. and Mrs. Prancer," he said, pulling us both into a hug. "How was the human ceremony?"

"Perfect," Kayla said. "My dad cried. My aunt got drunk and told embarrassing stories. The aurora appeared over London."

Nix appeared from the shadows, elegant as always. "The Council was quite impressed. The land doesn't usually respond so strongly outside the Arctic."

"It approved," I said simply, remembering the wonder on Kayla's face when she'd seen the northern lights blazing above the grey London sky.

Magnus clapped my shoulder. "Come on. Santa's waiting topside with half the magical community. Word got out about the bonding ceremony, and everyone wants to witness."

We climbed the stairs from the portal chamber to the main campus, and I felt Kayla tense beside me as we emerged into the open. The university grounds were transformed, ice sculptures lined every pathway, enchanted snow fell in gentle spirals, and magical lanterns floated through the air, casting warm golden light. But it was the crowd that made me catch my breath.

Hundreds of creatures packed the spaces between buildings. Shifters and sprites, elves and frost giants, even a few selkies who'd traveled from the coast. The entire North Pole community, it seemed, had gathered to witness our bond.

"Connor," Kayla whispered, gripping my hand tighter. "There are so many."

"They're here for us," I murmured back. "For what we represent. Human and shifter, choosing each other in front of the magic itself."

Santa waited at the edge of the Sacred Grounds, resplendent

in formal robes embroidered with silver thread. He smiled when he saw us. "Kayla, Connor. Welcome home. Are you ready to complete your bond?"

"Yes, sir," we said in unison.

"The ceremony will take place at sunset, approximately two hours from now. That gives you time to rest and prepare." His eyes twinkled, though something serious lingered beneath the warmth. "Your friends have been eagerly awaiting your return."

As if summoned, our NPU crew appeared, Rowan and Ivy, Elian and Fiona, Oliver standing slightly apart but present, and Sally Dancer wearing what could only be described as ceremonial sleigh harness finery, practically glowing with pride in her new role as lead reindeer.

"You're back!" Ivy threw herself at Kayla, pulling her into a hug.

"How was London? We heard the aurora appeared over the city, is that true?"

"It appeared," Kayla confirmed, laughing.

"My family couldn't believe it. My mom cried through the entire ceremony."

"As any proper mother should," Ivy said, pulling Kayla into a gentler hug. "Tonight will be different, though. More magical. More... visceral."

I caught the slight warning in her tone. The bonding ceremony wasn't just pretty words and exchanged rings. It was ancient magic, witnessed by the land itself, and it would mark us both permanently. Bond marks that would appear on our wrists, visible proof of our connection.

"We're ready," I assured her.

But was I? The question surfaced unbidden as the women whisked Kayla away and I watched her disappear into the preparation lodge. What if something went wrong? What if the magic rejected us despite everything we'd proven? What if Kayla saw my true form in the sacred circle and it was too much, not intellectually, but viscerally, in that moment when ancient power stripped away all pretense?

"Stop spiraling," Magnus said quietly, appearing at my elbow. "I can see it from here."

"I'm not..."

"You are." He steered me toward the male preparation lodge. "Come on. Let's get you ready before you talk yourself into a panic."

Inside the lodge, warmth from enchanted braziers chased away the cold. Sally was already there, along with Rowan, Elian, and Oliver. The space smelled of pine and magic, grounding and ancient all at once.

"Nervous?" Sally asked, offering me a flask of something that smelled like cinnamon and fire.

"Terrified," I admitted, taking a sip. The liquid burned pleasantly down my throat, warming me from the inside.

"Good." Oliver, surprisingly, was the one who spoke. "Fear means you understand the gravity of what you're doing. This isn't a human ceremony that can be undone with paperwork. Magical bonds are forever."

"I know." I met his stern gaze steadily. "I want forever with her."

Something shifted in Oliver's expression, approval, maybe, or respect. "Then you'll have it. The land will see to that."

Magnus pulled out formal robes for me, deep forest green embroidered with silver antlers and aurora patterns. They were heavier than I expected, lined with enchantments that would protect against the cold and enhance the ceremony's magic.

"These belonged to your father," Magnus said quietly. "He wore them when he bonded with your mother. I've been keeping them safe." He paused, his expression distant. "He stood in this same circle, years ago. Different crowd, same stakes."

My throat tightened. I took the robes carefully, feeling the weight of legacy and love woven into every thread. Dad had done this. Had stood before the altar with Mom, had let the pack witness their bond forming. And now I would follow that path, wearing his robes, carrying his memory into my own future.

"Thank you," I whispered.

As I dressed, Magnus explained what would happen. "The ceremony requires twelve reindeer shifters to form a circle around you and Kayla. We'll hold the space, channel the land's magic, witness the bond forming. Oliver will officiate, he's done this before, knows the old words."

"You'll need to shift at some point," Rowan added. "Show Kayla your true form within the sacred space. Let her touch you as reindeer, not just as human. That acceptance, her accepting all of you, is what seals the bond."

There it was again. That flutter of doubt in my chest.

"What if she hesitates?" The question escaped before I could stop it. "Not because she doesn't love me, but because the magic makes it different? Makes me different?"

The room went quiet.

"Then the bond doesn't form," Oliver said bluntly. "And you're no worse off than before. But Connor..." He stepped closer, his expression softer than I'd ever seen it. "That girl has faced down Oath Keeper trials designed to break humans. She's earned the respect of creatures who've lived for centuries. She chose you knowing exactly what you are. The ceremony doesn't change that. It just makes it official."

"The magic won't reject you," Magnus added. "I've seen how the aurora responds to you two. The land wants this bond. It's been celebrating it since the day you proposed."

I nodded, trying to internalize their confidence even as my own wavered.

The door to the lodge opened, and Santa stepped inside. The casual warmth from earlier was gone, replaced by something more formal, more ancient. This was Santa as magical authority, as keeper of North Pole traditions.

"It's nearly time," he said. "Connor, walk with me."

We stepped outside into the deepening twilight. The crowd was already gathering at the Sacred Grounds, hundreds of creatures finding positions around the ritual circle. I could see the twelve posts marking the perimeter, flames beginning to kindle atop each one.

"There will be some who watch tonight hoping to see you fail," Santa said quietly. "Not many, but enough to notice. Elders who believe the old ways should stay old. Council members who worry that bonds like yours will weaken magical bloodlines."

My jaw tightened. "You're telling me this now?"

"I'm telling you this so you're prepared." He stopped walking, turning to face me. "But Connor, I'm also telling you that I believe in what you and Kayla represent. The future isn't about purity or separation. It's about bridges. About choosing connection over isolation." His eyes gleamed. "Prove them wrong. Not with words, but with the bond itself. Show them that love transcends categories."

"No pressure," I muttered.

He smiled. "You've handled worse pressure. And you won't be alone in that circle. You'll have Kayla. That's always been your strength."

We continued toward the Sacred Grounds as the sun touched the horizon. The crowd parted to let us through, and I felt the weight of hundreds of eyes. Most were warm, excited, supportive. But scattered among them were faces that watched without smiling, elders whose expressions held skepticism, doubt, maybe even disapproval.

The aurora began to wake overhead, ribbons of green and gold dancing against the darkening sky.

The Sacred Grounds had been transformed. Twelve posts marked a circle at the clearing's heart, each carved with ancient runes and topped with magical flames. In the center stood an altar, simple stone, worn smooth by centuries of ceremonies.

And there, waiting beside the altar in her enchanted wedding dress, was Kayla.

My breath stopped.

The dress that had looked elegant and subtle in London was waking now, responding to the North Pole's magic. The shimmer I'd barely noticed before blazed visible, silver threads running through the white silk like captured starlight. The crystal beading glowed softly, and the fabric itself seemed to pulse with light in time with her heartbeat.

She was ethereal. Otherworldly. And yet utterly herself, Kayla, my partner, made of grit and wonder.

But as I approached, I saw the tension in her shoulders. The way her hands trembled slightly at her sides.

"Hey," I said softly, taking her hands in mine. "You okay?"

"What if I don't feel it?" she whispered, her eyes wide with fear. "The bond. What if the magic doesn't work for me because I'm human? What if everyone's watching and nothing happens and we've built all this up for..."

"Kayla." I squeezed her hands, grounding her. "Look at me."

She did, her green eyes shining with unshed tears.

"The magic already works for you," I said firmly. "You survived the Oath Keeper trials. You wear an enchanted ring that leads you home to me. The aurora appeared over London at our wedding. The land has been approving of us since the beginning." I touched her cheek. "This ceremony doesn't create our bond. It just makes it visible."

"What if I mess it up?"

"You won't." I pulled her close, pressing my forehead to hers. "We won't. Together, remember?"

She took a shaky breath, then nodded. "Together."

Crystal appeared beside us, her own eyes damp. "Remember when you couldn't even pick a dress?" she said to Kayla with a watery smile. "Now look at you. About to walk into magical fire with a reindeer shifter who adores you."

Kayla laughed, the sound breaking through her fear. "I've come a long way from that dressing room."

"You both have," Crystal said, squeezing Kayla's shoulder before stepping back to join the crowd.

The witnesses settled into position around the circle's perimeter, creating a living wall. I saw Magnus and Nix standing together, Rowan and Ivy holding hands. Even the skeptical elders had moved closer, drawn by the power building in the air.

Santa stepped forward, his presence commanding attention without effort. "We gather tonight to witness something ancient and new. A bond between human and shifter, sealed under the aurora, blessed by the land itself." His gaze swept the crowd, lingering on the doubters. "Let all present understand: what the North Pole approves, no creature can deny."

A ripple moved through the assembled witnesses, acceptance from some, reluctant acknowledgment from others.

Oliver moved to stand before the altar, his expression solemn but not unkind. Behind him, the twelve reindeer shifters took their positions at the posts, Magnus, Sally, Rowan, Elian, and eight others from the sleigh teams. The moment they were in place, I felt magic shift in the air. Heavy. Ancient. Waiting.

The aurora blazed brighter, as if the land itself was leaning in to watch.

Oliver raised his hands, and absolute silence fell across the Sacred Grounds. Even the wind seemed to hold its breath.

"It's time," he said quietly, his eyes on me and Kayla. "Take your positions."

Kayla's hand found mine, our fingers interlacing. Her pulse hammered against my palm, matching my own racing heart.

This was it. The moment we'd been building toward since that first day in Intro to Sleigh Dynamics. Since the day a human girl had looked at me and seen not just a shifter heir, but a person worth knowing.

She'd crossed into this world one cautious step at a time. Tonight she was walking into fire.

CHAPTER SIX
THE BONDING CEREMONY
KAYLA

THE ALTAR STONE WAS COLD BENEATH MY PALMS, ANCIENT AND WORN smooth by centuries of ceremonies just like this one. Except not like this one at all, because how many humans had stood here, about to be bonded to a reindeer shifter under the witness of the North Pole itself?

My dress pulsed with light, the enchantments fully awake now. I could feel magic humming through the silk, responding to the power building in the Sacred Grounds. It was overwhelming and beautiful and terrifying all at once.

Oliver's voice rang out in the old language, words I didn't understand but felt in my bones. The twelve reindeer shifters at the circle's posts began to chant, low and rhythmic, and the sound vibrated through the ground and up through my legs. The aurora overhead blazed brighter with each syllable, as if the sky itself was listening.

Connor stood beside me, his father's robes making him look every inch the heir he'd been born to be. But his hand found mine, our fingers interlacing, and I felt his pulse racing as fast as my own.

We were both terrified, but ready.

"Connor Prancer," Oliver said, switching to common tongue. "Step forward and show your truth."

Connor squeezed my hand once, then released it. He moved to the center of the circle, directly beneath the aurora's brightest point. The crowd pressed closer, hundreds of eyes watching. I saw the skeptical elders, their faces unreadable. Saw Crystal gripping Magnus's arm. Saw Santa standing tall and steady.

Then Connor began to shift.

I'd seen it before, of course I had. But never like this. Never surrounded by ancient magic that made every transformation sacred, that stripped away pretense and showed truth in its rawest form.

His form blurred, expanded. One moment he stood on two legs in forest-green robes, the next he was magnificent, antlers spreading wide, powerful shoulders, dark eyes that held Connor's intelligence but in a body that was purely, undeniably other.

The flames atop the twelve posts flared higher. The aurora blazed so bright I had to squint against the light. Magic pressed against my skin like a physical weight, and my dress responded, the enchantments blazing brighter until I was wrapped in silver-white light.

"Kayla Matthews," Oliver intoned. "Approach your intended. Look upon his truth and choose."

This was it. The moment everything hinged on.

I took a step forward on shaking legs. The magic intensified with my movement, swirling around me, through me. I could taste it, winter wind and pine, ancient snow and starlight. My wrists burned where I knew the bond marks waited to form, held back only by my acceptance or rejection.

Connor, the reindeer, lowered his massive head, giving me access, trusting me completely. His breath came out in visible puffs of frost that dissipated into the charged air.

I could feel the crowd holding its breath. Could sense their doubt and hope, and curiosity all tangled together. But all of that faded when I looked into Connor's eyes.

Still him. Still my partner who wanted to build impossible dreams with me. Just... more.

I reached out, my hand trembling, and touched his muzzle.

The world exploded.

Magic flooded through me, not gentle, not gradual, but a torrent of power that lit up every nerve ending. I gasped, nearly stumbled, but Connor pressed forward slightly, steadying me with his solid presence. Where my skin met his fur, golden light spiraled up my arm in intricate patterns that matched the aurora overhead.

The bond mark appeared on my wrist, not painted on, but emerging from within, like it had always been there waiting to be revealed. Gold that shimmered and pulsed, warm beneath my skin, alive with magic I could finally feel instead of just observe.

"Hello," I whispered through tears I didn't remember starting to cry.

The magic surged again, and this time I didn't fight it. I let it wash through me, let it show me what Connor felt, his love, his fear, his desperate hope that I would accept him, his relief when I did. I felt his joy crash into mine, felt our emotions tangle and merge until I couldn't tell where mine ended and his began.

The dress transformed.

The subtle shimmer that had been barely visible exploded into brilliance. Silver threads blazed like captured lightning, the crystal beading erupting into points of light that rivaled the stars. The fabric itself seemed to come alive, moving with magic instead of just wind, and I felt the enchantments settle into my skin like a second layer of blessing.

I looked like magic incarnate. Felt like it too.

Connor shifted back to human form, the transformation smooth and quick. He caught me as my knees buckled, steadying me against his chest. His robes had reformed, but now they carried traces of the same golden light that marked our wrists.

"I feel you," I gasped, my hand pressed over my heart where his emotions now lived alongside my own. "Inside. Connor, I can feel..."

"I know." His voice was wrecked, raw with emotion. "I feel you too."

The bond wasn't just enchantment. It was intimacy. Connection. A presence woven into my own, his joy becoming my joy, his love a constant warmth beneath my ribs. When I looked up at him, I knew he felt the same from me.

CONNOR

The bond was everything.

Not an abstract concept or a pretty tradition, it was real and visceral and so intense I could barely breathe through it. Kayla's emotions flooded through our connection: wonder and joy and a thread of lingering fear that was already dissolving into certainty. Her love wrapped around my heart like a physical embrace.

The mark on my wrist blazed gold, matching hers exactly, intricate patterns that echoed the aurora, permanent proof of what we'd chosen. Not just visible on the surface, but embedded in my very being. I would carry this mark, this bond, for the rest of my life.

Forever suddenly felt like the perfect amount of time.

Oliver stepped forward, approval clear in his stern features. "The marks have appeared. The bond has formed. Now speak your vows in the old way, that the land may witness and seal what you have chosen."

He produced a ceremonial blade, silver and ancient, etched with runes that glowed softly in the aurora light. This was the final piece of the ritual, the symbolic severing of old paths to make way for the new one we'd build together.

Oliver held out a length of silver cord, stretching it taut between his hands. "This cord represents the separate paths you walked before this moment. To complete the bond, you must sever the past and choose the future together."

I looked at Kayla, at my wife who glowed with magic and determination. *Are you ready?*

Her answer came through the bond before she spoke: *Yes. Always yes.*

Together, we gripped the blade's hilt, her hand over mine, our bond marks pressed together and flaring brighter at the contact. The connection between us intensified until I could feel her heartbeat as clearly as my own, until I couldn't tell where my magic ended and hers began.

"Speak your intention," Oliver commanded.

"I sever the path I walked alone," I said, my voice carrying across the Sacred Grounds with a strength I hadn't known I possessed. "I choose the path we build together."

"I sever the path I walked alone," Kayla echoed, her voice just as strong. "I choose the path we build together."

We brought the blade down as one.

The cord parted with a sound like breaking ice, and magic detonated through the circle. Not violent, overwhelming. A wave of power that made the crowd gasp and step back, that sent the flames atop the twelve posts shooting twenty feet into the air, that made the aurora overhead blaze so bright it was like daylight in the Sacred Grounds.

The bond marks on our wrists pulsed once, twice, three times, each pulse sending another surge of magic through both of us. Then they settled, the glow fading until the marks were visible but no longer luminous. Permanent. Real. Ours.

I pulled Kayla close, crushing her against my chest, feeling the bond hum between us like a living thing. She was crying and laughing simultaneously, clinging to me like I was her anchor in the aftermath of so much power.

"We did it," she whispered against my neck. "Connor, we actually did it."

"Did you doubt?" I pulled back enough to see her face, to watch aurora light paint her features in gold and green.

"Maybe a little." She smiled through her tears, radiant and beautiful and mine. "Not anymore."

Oliver raised his hands, and the crowd fell silent one last time. "By the power of the North Pole, witnessed by the land and aurora, sealed by ancient magic and present choice, I declare Connor Prancer and Kayla Matthews bonded." His voice rang with finality and triumph. "What the magic has joined, no mortal force can separate."

The crowd erupted.

Cheers and howls filled the Sacred Grounds. Sprites launched themselves into aerial displays, leaving trails of colored light. Reindeer shifters stamped their approval, the sound like thunder. Even most of the skeptical elders were nodding, acknowledging what they'd witnessed, a bond so strong the land itself had responded with unprecedented power.

The aurora continued its brilliant dance, celebrating with us.

Magnus reached us first, pulling us both into a crushing hug. "That was incredible," he said, his voice thick with emotion. "Your father would be so proud, Connor. So damn proud."

"The bond marks," Nix breathed, taking Kayla's wrist gently to examine the intricate patterns. "I've never seen them this detailed. The magic really approved."

Crystal threw herself at Kayla, both of them dissolving into happy tears. Rowan and Ivy offered elegant congratulations, their own bond marks visible on their wrists, proof that they understood exactly what we'd just experienced. Elian and Fiona beamed. Sally clapped my shoulder and made a joke that had Oliver glaring at him, though I caught the slight smile the old reindeer tried to hide.

Through it all, I kept one hand on Kayla, maintaining physical contact, marveling at the bond that now connected us in ways that went beyond touch.

Tables appeared across the Sacred Grounds, conjured by magic or prepared in advance, I wasn't sure which. Food materialized, drinks flowed, and music filled the air as a sprite ensemble began to play. The solemn ritual transformed into a joyous celebration, and we were swept up in it.

Santa approached with two small boxes. "A wedding gift," he said warmly. "Or rather, two."

He opened the first box to reveal two keys identical to the one he'd given us earlier. "One for each of you. You'll build the academy together, lead it together. These ensure you both have equal authority."

The second box held two delicate circlets, silver bands etched with runes and set with small crystals that caught the aurora light. They were beautiful but understated, clearly ceremonial but not ostentatious.

"These mark you as recognized leaders in the magical community," Santa explained. "Wear them when you represent the academy, when you meet with the Council. They carry the North Pole's full endorsement."

Kayla touched one of the circlets carefully, and I felt her awe through the bond. "Thank you," she whispered.

"You've earned them." Santa's eyes twinkled. "Both of you. Now go, celebrate. Tomorrow the real work begins, but tonight is for joy."

As the celebration continued around us, friends danced, magical fireworks exploded overhead, and the aurora painted everything in shifting colors. Kayla and I found ourselves at the circle's edge, watching.

"I can feel you," she said quietly, wonder in her voice. "All the time. Your emotions, your presence. It's not intrusive, it's like you're part of my foundation now."

"Same," I admitted, pulling her closer. "It's strange and perfect and exactly right."

She leaned her head on my shoulder. "We're building something that will outlast us, Connor. Something that changes everything."

"One bridge at a time," I murmured, pressing a kiss to her temple.

Movement at the forest edge caught my eye, two figures watching from the shadows. An elf and a sprite, their expressions unreadable. When they noticed me looking, they melted back into the trees.

A whisper of unease threaded through the bond, and I knew Kayla had seen them too.

"Not everyone's celebrating," she said quietly.

"No." I tightened my arm around her waist. "But we knew that. Santa warned us."

"We'll prove them wrong," Kayla said with quiet determination. "Just like we did tonight."

"Just like we did tonight," I agreed.

The aurora blazed overhead, and I chose to trust that instead of the shadows. We'd proven our bond was real, that human and shifter could be joined by something stronger than tradition or blood. We'd shown the magical community that love could transcend categories, that bridges could be built across any divide.

But proving it once wasn't the same as changing centuries of belief.

That work started tomorrow.

Tonight was for celebration. For holding my wife close and feeling our bond hum between us like a promise written in starlight. For dancing under the aurora with our pack and friends surrounding us. For joy.

"Dance with me?" Kayla asked, tugging me toward where others swayed to the music.

I took her hand and we moved together under the blazing aurora, our bond marks glowing softly in the darkness, our forever officially begun.

CHAPTER SEVEN
REALITY SETS IN

KAYLA

Morning came too early and too bright.

I woke in Connor's arms in the guest quarters Santa had arranged for us, sunlight, actual sunlight, rare at the North Pole, streaming through the window. The bond hummed pleasantly between us, a warm, constant presence that told me Connor was still asleep, his dreams peaceful and content.

My wrist caught the light, and I turned it slowly, watching the bond mark shimmer beneath my skin. Gold patterns that echoed the aurora, permanent and beautiful. Proof that last night hadn't been a dream.

We were bonded. Married in both worlds. And today, reality would catch up with the celebration.

Connor stirred beside me, his arm tightening around my waist. "Morning," he mumbled against my hair. Through the bond, I felt his contentment, his love, and beneath it, a thread of nervousness about what came next.

"Morning." I turned in his arms to face him. "Ready to build a school?"

He laughed softly. "Ask me after coffee."

But there would be no leisurely morning. A knock at the door came precisely at eight, and Santa's voice carried through the wood. "Kayla, Connor. When you're ready, I have something to show you."

Twenty minutes later, we stood in Santa's office alongside Magnus and Elder Frost. The circlets from last night's ceremony sat on Santa's desk, gleaming in the morning light, a reminder of the authority and responsibility we'd accepted.

"The academy site," Santa said without preamble, spreading a large map across his desk. "I thought you should see the actual land this morning. Before the romance of the bonding ceremony fades and reality sets in."

I leaned forward, studying the map. The site was marked on the eastern edge of North Pole territory, currently empty land, bordered by forest on one side and open tundra on the other.

Connor's hand found mine, our bond marks warm where they touched. "How long do we have?"

"Construction begins next week," Elder Frost said crisply. "The Council has approved the budget and hired contractors. But the timeline is aggressive, we're aiming to open for students next fall. That gives you approximately eleven months to build the physical campus, develop curriculum, hire staff, and establish all operational protocols."

Eleven months. To build an entire school from nothing.

Through the bond, I felt Connor's surge of panic match my own.

"The good news," Magnus added, clearly trying to be encouraging, "is that you won't be alone. The Council is assigning advisors. Some of the NPU faculty have agreed to consult. And you'll have each other."

"The challenges," Elder Frost continued, her tone practical, "are significant. You'll need to balance human and magical curricula. Determine which courses are mandatory versus elective. Decide on housing arrangements, do you separate human and creature students, or integrate them from day one? Establish safety protocols. Hire faculty who can teach mixed classrooms. And you'll need to do all of this while navigating Council politics and community resistance."

"Resistance?" I asked, though I already knew the answer. I'd seen those elders watching last night, their expressions skeptical.

"Not everyone supports this academy," Santa reminded us gently. "Some believe magical education should remain purely magical. Others worry that integrating human children will dilute our traditions or compromise security. You proved your bond last night, proved that human and shifter can join. But that doesn't mean everyone believes an entire institution should be built on that principle."

Connor's jaw tightened. "So we'll prove them wrong again."

"You'll try," Elder Frost corrected. "But understand, this academy is an experiment. If it fails, it sets back integration efforts by decades. The Council is watching. The community is watching. And some of them are hoping you'll fail so they can say, 'See? We told you it wouldn't work.'"

The weight of that settled over me like a physical thing. Not just building a school. Building a school that had to succeed, that couldn't afford to fail, that carried the hopes and fears of an entire movement on its shoulders.

"When do we see the site?" Connor asked.

Santa smiled. "Right now, if you're ready."

THE PORTAL DEPOSITED us on a snow-covered plain that stretched endlessly in all directions.

Empty. Completely, utterly empty.

"This is it?" I asked, turning in a slow circle. There was nothing here, no buildings, no markers, just virgin snow and distant tree line.

"This is it," Santa confirmed. He gestured broadly. "Forty acres. Enough for classroom buildings, dormitories, administrative offices, recreational facilities, and room to grow."

I tried to envision it. Tried to see buildings where there was only snow, students where there was only silence, a thriving campus where there was only potential.

"It's perfect," Connor said quietly.

I looked at him. "It's empty."

"Exactly." He squeezed my hand, and through the bond I felt his excitement building. "It's not weighed down by centuries of tradition or expectations. We can build it exactly how we want. Make it what students need, not what it's always been."

Magnus nodded approvingly. "That's the right perspective."

But as I stood there in the vast emptiness, reality crashed over me in waves. We had to build this. Not just imagine it or plan it, actually build it. Eleven months to create something from nothing, to establish an institution that would change lives, to prove that our vision wasn't just romantic idealism but practical reality.

"Where do we even start?" I whispered.

Santa pulled a thick folder from inside his coat. "With this. Initial architectural plans, budget breakdowns, contractor schedules, curriculum frameworks. It's not comprehensive, you'll need to make thousands of decisions. But it's a foundation."

Connor took the folder, his expression determined. I felt his resolve through the bond, his willingness to dive into the impossible and figure it out as we went.

But I also felt my own doubt creeping in. What if we couldn't do this? What if we'd agreed to something too big, too complex, too important to trust to two twenty-three-year-olds fresh out of university?

"You're spiraling," Connor murmured, pulling me close. "I can feel it."

"We've never done this before," I said quietly. "Built a school. Run an institution. We barely know what we're doing."

"True." He pressed a kiss to my temple. "But we've never done a lot of things before we did them. You'd never survived Oath Keeper trials until you did. I'd never broken flight records until I did. We'd never bonded a human and shifter until last night." He turned me to face him. "We figure it out together. One impossible thing at a time."

Santa cleared his throat. "If I may, the Council chose you precisely because you don't know what you're doing."

I blinked at him. "That's supposed to be encouraging?"

"It is." His eyes twinkled. "Experienced educators would build what they know. They'd replicate existing structures, fall back on traditional methods. You two will build something new because you don't know any better. You'll make mistakes, certainly. But you'll also innovate in ways people entrenched in the old systems never could."

Elder Frost actually smiled, a rare sight. "You're bridge builders. You proved that at NPU. Now you just have to build a bigger bridge."

Magnus gestured to the empty land. "Picture it. Where do you want the main building?"

Connor and I looked at each other, then at the blank canvas before us. Slowly, he pointed toward a slight rise in the land. "There. Where students can see the aurora clearly. Where the building feels like part of the landscape instead of imposed on it."

"Dormitories flanking it," I added, catching his vision. "Close enough for community but separate enough for quiet. And maybe..." I turned, looking toward the tree line. "A grove for outdoor classes. Magical theory needs practical application."

"Library in the center," Connor continued, his excitement growing. "Making knowledge the heart of everything."

Santa was nodding. Magnus grinned. Even Elder Frost looked pleased.

"See?" Santa said. "You're already building it."

But as the morning wore on and Santa walked us through the practical realities , smaller budgets than I'd hoped, tighter time- lines than seemed possible, and staffing challenges with no easy solutions , my doubt crept back.

"We're going to fail," I said quietly as we stood alone in the center of the empty site, Santa and the others having stepped away to discuss construction logistics.

Connor turned to me. "Maybe."

I stared at him. "That's not the pep talk I was hoping for."

"But if we fail," he continued, "we'll fail together. Building something we believed in. Trying to make the world better." He cupped my face in his hands. "And Kayla? I don't think we're going to fail. I think we're going to build something extraordinary. Because we always have."

Through the bond, I felt his absolute certainty. His unwa- vering belief not just in the vision, but in us. In our partnership. In our ability to figure out the impossible.

"One bridge at a time," I said and he nodded.

I took a deep breath, looking at the empty land with fresh

eyes. Not empty, full of potential. Not overwhelming, an opportunity.

"Okay," I said. "Let's build a school."

Connor pulled me close, and standing in the center of forty acres of nothing, surrounded by the enormity of what we'd agreed to do, I felt the bond between us steady and strong.

CHAPTER EIGHT
THE FUTURE TAKES SHAPE

CONNOR

The packages started arriving the over the next few days.

I found the first one outside our temporary quarters, a thick envelope from Magnus with a Council seal. Inside: staffing recommendations, curriculum proposals, and a note in his precise handwriting: *You'll need faculty who believe in the mission. These are the ones I trust. Also flagged one who might be trouble; your call.*

"What's that?" Kayla asked, appearing in the doorway with two cups of coffee.

"Magnus sent teacher recommendations." I spread the documents across our small kitchen table. "He's been busy."

Kayla set down the coffee and picked up the top page, scanning the names. Her finger stopped on one entry marked with a red asterisk. "Soren Coldbrook. 'Qualified but has expressed concerns about preserving traditional magical education.' Why would Magnus recommend someone who sounds like a purist?"

"He added a note." I pointed to the margin. *Better to know who might cause problems than be blindsided later. Your academy, your choice.*

Through the bond, I felt Kayla's uncertainty mirror my own. "Do we hire someone who might undermine us?"

"Do we exclude someone before giving them a chance?" I countered. "Maybe teaching integrated classes will change his mind."

"Or maybe he'll poison students against the whole concept." Kayla sighed, setting down the page. "This is harder than I thought. Every decision has consequences."

A knock interrupted us. Kayla opened the door to find a delivery sprite hovering with a rolled set of plans nearly as large as she was.

"From Rowan Blackthorn and Ivy Snowfall," the sprite announced in a voice like tinkling bells. "They said to tell you: 'Beauty and function, no compromises.'"

The sprite deposited the plans and zipped away before we could respond.

Kayla and I unrolled the architectural drawings across the floor, weighting the corners with books and coffee mugs. The designs were stunning, curved buildings that flowed with the landscape, circular classrooms for collaboration, hexagonal spaces for focused study. Nothing like the rigid rectangles of traditional North Pole architecture.

"It's gorgeous," Kayla breathed, tracing one of the flowing lines with her finger.

"It's expensive," I said, noting the materials list. Enchanted glass that responded to magical signatures. Adaptive temperature controls for different creature comforts. Flexible walls that could expand or contract based on class size.

"It's exactly what we need." Kayla looked up at me, determination in her green eyes. "This building tells students they belong. That the academy was designed for them, not despite them."

A note fluttered from between the plans, written in Ivy's flowing script:

We'll teach one course per semester if you'll have us. Magical Architecture and Integration Design. The building itself will be the textbook. Also, Rowan ran the numbers. It's buildable in your timeline if the contractors start next week. Expensive, but worth it.

Trust us. Trust the vision.

- Ivy & Rowan

"We're going to be over budget before we even start," I said, though I was already imagining students learning in those spaces.

"Then we find more budget." Kayla rolled up the plans carefully. "Magnus and Nix can help navigate Council funding. This is too important to compromise."

My tablet chimed with an incoming message. I glanced at the screen and felt warmth spread through my chest.

"Elian and Fiona," I said, reading aloud. "They're offering guest lectures. One week per semester on global integration efforts. They want to show students that what we're building isn't just theory, it's already happening around the world."

Kayla moved to read over my shoulder. "Finnish forest sprites working with Norwegian frost giants. Scottish selkies partnering with human marine biologists." She smiled. "Real-world applications. That's perfect."

"They can't commit full-time," I continued reading. "But they want to contribute. Show students the bigger picture."

"Everyone wants to help," Kayla said softly. "Magnus sending recommendations. Rowan and Ivy redesigning the entire campus. Elian and Fiona offering their expertise." Her voice wavered slightly. "We're not doing this alone."

I pulled her close, feeling the bond hum between us. "We never were. That's the whole point, isn't it? Building something that requires all of us."

The rest of the morning brought more messages. Nix sent a detailed curriculum proposal that wove sprite magical history alongside traditional reindeer and elf teachings. Three NPU professors agreed to teach part-time courses. Sally Dancer, still buzzing with pride over her new lead position, volunteered to coach the academy's flight team once students were ready.

By afternoon, our small quarters looked like a campaign head-quarters. Papers covered every surface, plans tacked to walls, lists of decisions multiplying faster than we could address them.

"We need a system," Kayla said, surveying the chaos. "Some way to track everything."

"We need an office," I corrected. "And staff. And about six more hours in each day."

She laughed, the sound slightly manic. "Is it too late to back out?"

"Absolutely." I kissed her temple. "We're committed now. Besides, look at all this support. We'd disappoint everyone."

"No pressure."

"Immense pressure." I grinned. "But we've handled worse."

KAYLA

Evening brought unexpected visitors.

I answered the knock to find two elderly Council members standing in the hallway, Theo Evergreen, an elf whose silver hair seemed to shimmer with its own light, and Eira Starweaver, a sprite whose presence made the air feel charged with electricity.

"May we come in?" Theo asked, his ancient eyes kind but serious.

Connor appeared at my shoulder. "Of course. Please."

They entered, and I hastily cleared space on the sofa, shoving architectural plans aside. Theo and Eira settled with the grace of beings who'd lived for centuries, their movements economical and precise.

"We won't keep you long," Theo began. "But we felt you should know, the Council isn't united in supporting this academy."

My stomach dropped. "We know there's skepticism."

"Not skepticism." Eira's voice was sharp as winter wind. "Opposition. Organized, strategic opposition from members who believe the old ways should remain old."

Connor's hand found mine, our bond marks warming where they touched. "What do they want?"

"For you to fail," Theo said bluntly. "Or more precisely, for you to provide an excuse they can use to shut the academy down. Poor enrollment. Safety incidents. Academic failures. Anything they can frame as proof that integration doesn't work at the institutional level."

Through the bond, I felt Connor's anger rising to match my own. We'd known this wouldn't be easy, but hearing it stated so plainly made the threat feel immediate.

"Why are you telling us this?" I asked.

Theo and Eira exchanged a glance. Then Eira leaned forward, her expression intense. "Because we don't want you to fail. We believe this academy is necessary. But you need to understand what you're facing."

"Build something so strong they can't tear it down," Theo continued. "Be so careful they can't find legitimate criticism.

Succeed so thoroughly that even your opponents must acknowledge it works."

"No pressure," I muttered, echoing my earlier comment to Connor.

"Immense pressure," Eira agreed, though her lips quirked slightly. "But you're not alone. There are Council members who support you. Who will defend your work when critics attack. You just need to give us something worth defending."

They stood to leave, but Theo paused at the door. "One more thing. The resistance you'll face, it's not personal. It's fear. Fear that change will erase traditions they've spent lifetimes protecting. Show them that evolution doesn't mean erasure. That honoring the past and building the future aren't mutually exclusive."

After they left, Connor and I sat in silence, processing.

"Well," Connor finally said. "That was terrifying."

"And clarifying." I looked at the paperwork surrounding us, the support from our friends, the plans and proposals and offers to help. "We have allies. Real ones. Magnus, Nix, Rowan, Ivy, Elian, Fiona. Theo and Eira. Even Sally, in her way."

"And we have opponents," Connor added.

"Then we'll be better." I stood, pulling him up with me. "We'll be so good at this, so careful and thorough and successful, that even the purists can't deny it works."

Connor wrapped his arms around me, and I leaned into his solid presence. Through the bond, I felt his fear and determination, his love and his resolve. We were in this together, building something bigger than either of us, something that would outlast us.

"Tomorrow we start making real decisions," I said. "Reviewing Magnus's candidates. Choosing between Rowan's ambitious designs and more practical options. Figuring out budgets and timelines and all the impossible logistics."

Connor kissed me, slow and sweet, tasting of coffee and determination and the future we were choosing. When we finally broke apart, the paperwork didn't seem quite as overwhelming.

We had support. We had opposition. We had eleven months to build something extraordinary.

CHAPTER NINE
BRIDGES FOR THE NEXT GENERATION

CONNOR

The empty academy site looked different this morning.

Perhaps it was the early light that painted the snow in shades of rose and gold. Maybe it was knowing that tomorrow, contractors would break ground and the emptiness would start filling with something real. Or maybe it was simply that Kayla stood beside me, our bond marks warm where our hands joined, and everything looked different through that lens.

"One tree," she said, pulling a small sapling from the enchanted carrying case Santa had provided. "One symbolic first act before the chaos starts."

The tree was barely three feet tall, a northern pine with needles that shimmered faintly with preservation magic. According to the greenhouse keeper who'd grown it, the tree would thrive in the harsh arctic climate and grow for centuries if properly planted.

"Where?" I asked.

Kayla walked slowly across the site, her boots crunching in

the snow. She stopped at the center point, where Ivy's plans showed a courtyard between the main building and dormitories. "Here. Where students will pass every day. Where they'll see it grow as they grow."

I started clearing snow, digging down to frozen earth. The ground was hard, resistant, but I kept at it, using a combination of physical effort and careful warming magic to soften the soil. Kayla knelt beside me, her hands joining mine in the work.

"My dad planted a tree when I was born," she said quietly. "In our backyard in London. He said trees are patient teachers, they show you that growth takes time, that strong foundations matter, that storms pass but roots remain."

"Wise man, your father." I finally broke through the frozen layer to darker, richer soil beneath.

Together, we positioned the sapling carefully, packing earth around its roots. Kayla whispered something, a blessing in Mandarin that her grandmother had taught her, while I added a thread of winter magic to help the tree acclimate.

When we finished, we sat back on our heels, looking at the small tree standing alone in the vast emptiness.

"It looks fragile," Kayla said.

"It looks determined," I countered. "Like it knows it belongs here."

She leaned against me, and through the bond I felt her emotions, hope and fear tangled together, love for what we were building mixed with terror that we'd fail. But underneath it all, resolve. Steady and unshakeable.

"Twelve years from now," I said, "this tree will be taller than us. And students will sit under it studying, complaining about exams, falling in love, planning their futures."

"Your future students," Kayla added. "Our legacy."

"No." I turned her to face me. "Their legacy. We're just building the foundation. They'll build everything else."

KAYLA

Connor's words settled into my chest like a promise.

We weren't building this academy for ourselves, not really. We were building it for the eleven-year-old who'd arrive next fall, uncertain if they belonged. For the sprite who'd never had human friends before. For the reindeer shifter, learning to see humans as equals. For every student who'd walk through doors we hadn't even built yet.

"I'm terrified," I admitted, staring at the lone tree in the empty field. "What if we can't do this? What if the purists are right and integration doesn't scale? What if..."

"Hey." Connor cupped my face, his thumbs brushing away tears I hadn't realized were falling. "We survived four years at NPU being told we couldn't bond. We proved everyone wrong. We'll do it again."

"That was just us. This is..."

"Bigger," he agreed. "Scarier. More important." He pressed his forehead to mine. "And we're not doing it alone. We have Magnus and Nix. Rowan and Ivy. Elian and Fiona. Santa. The Council members who believe. Our pack."

Through the bond, I felt his certainty wash over my fear, not erasing it but tempering it, making it manageable.

"What if our kids come here someday?" I asked quietly. "What if we're building the school where our own children will learn?"

Connor's eyes widened slightly. We hadn't talked much about children yet, too focused on weddings and academies and surviving the present to think seriously about that future. But I felt his joy spike through the bond at the thought.

"Then we better build it right," he said softly. "Because I want them to see what's possible when you refuse to accept limitations others try to impose."

A cold wind swept across the empty site, making the small tree's branches shiver. But it held, roots already taking hold in the frozen ground.

"We should go," I said, checking my watch. "Magnus is meeting us in an hour to go over final contractor agreements."

Connor stood, pulling me up with him. But he paused, looking back at the tree one more time. "You know what we should do? When students arrive next fall, we should tell them about this tree. About how it was the first thing we planted. About how it represents the academy's mission."

"Growth takes time," I said, echoing my father's words. "Strong foundations matter. Storms pass but roots remain."

"Exactly." Connor squeezed my hand, our bond marks pulsing with warmth. "Come on, Director. We have an academy to build."

CONNOR

The next eleven months stretched before us like an impossible mountain to climb.

But standing there with Kayla, looking at the small tree we'd planted together in the empty field, I didn't feel overwhelmed. I felt ready.

We'd start with one decision. Then another. One classroom, one policy, one teacher, one student at a time. We'd make mistakes, definitely. We'd face opposition, certainly. We'd doubt ourselves, probably daily.

But we'd do it together.

The aurora began to wake overhead early this morning, with ribbons of green and gold dancing across the morning sky. Our bond marks caught the light, glowing faintly in response.

"The land approves," Kayla said, wonder in her voice.

"The land's been approving since the day I proposed," I reminded her. "It knows what we're capable of before we do."

She turned to face me fully, and I saw in her expression everything I loved, her courage and doubt, her brilliance and uncertainty, her absolute refusal to give up even when terrified.

"Promise me something," she said.

"Anything."

"Promise that when this gets hard, when the Council pushes back, when construction falls behind, when nothing works like we planned, promise we'll remember this moment. This tree. This feeling of possibility."

I pulled her close, wrapping my arms around her as the aurora blazed brighter overhead. "I promise. And Kayla? When we doubt ourselves, when we wonder if we're enough, we'll remember we built bridges that weren't supposed to exist. We bonded when they said it was impossible. We belong to each other and to this mission."

"Some bridges take a lifetime to build," she whispered against my chest.

"Lucky we're just getting started," I said.

The tree stood behind us, small but determined, already part of the landscape. Tomorrow, construction would begin. Walls would rise. Rooms would take shape. An academy would emerge from nothing, one stone at a time.

But today was for this, for standing in the empty field with my wife, for planting something that would outlast us, for choosing hope over fear.

The aurora danced above, the frozen ground held our tree's roots, and the future waited to be built.

I looked at the site one last time, empty now, but not for long. Soon it would be filled with voices and magic, with students learning to build their own bridges, with the next generation discovering what was possible when difference became foundation instead of obstacle.

EPILOGUE: TWELVE YEARS LATER

The northern pine was now taller than Connor.

He stood beneath its branches in the academy courtyard, watching the evening settle over the campus, with its curved buildings that followed the landscape's natural flow, and students moving between classes, their laughter echoing across the spaces he and Kayla had built from nothing. Twelve years. Sometimes it felt like yesterday they'd planted this tree in an empty field. Other times, it felt like a lifetime ago.

"Dad!" Cole's voice carried across the courtyard. "Mom says dinner's in ten minutes and if you're late again, she's giving your dessert to Holly!"

Connor grinned at his nine-year-old son, who was currently stuck mid-shift, antlers half-formed, one leg still human while the other had fur.

It was too soon for him to be turning. Most shifters had their first shift when they hit puberty. But most shifters weren't half-human. It was one of the reasons they had created the Academy and were living at the North Pole. Holly had had her first shift only months ago.

"Need help?"

"I've got it," Cole insisted, his face scrunched in concentration. A moment later, he completed the shift to full reindeer form, then immediately shifted back, stumbling slightly. "See? Totally got it."

"Very smooth," Connor said diplomatically, ruffling his son's hair as they walked toward the Headmaster's residence, a modest building at the campus edge that served as both home and office.

Inside, Kayla was setting the table while Holly, their eleven-year-old daughter, complained about her upcoming placement exam for the academy's secondary program. She'd be starting seventh grade in the fall, the first of their children to attend the school her parents had built.

"Everyone's going to expect me to be perfect because you're the Headmaster," Holly said, her dark hair, so like Kayla's, falling across her face as she aggressively folded napkins. "It's a lot."

"No one expects perfection," Kayla said gently. "They expect you to try your best."

"That's basically the same thing."

Connor caught Kayla's eye across the table and felt her amusement through their bond. Their daughter had inherited her mother's determination and her father's stubborn streak, a combination that would either change the world or drive her teachers to early retirement.

After dinner, after Cole and Holly were settled with homework, Connor knocked on Holly's door.

"Come in," she called, looking up from where she sat cross-legged on her bed, surrounded by textbooks.

Connor settled beside her. "Want to talk about it? The real worry, not the 'everyone expects perfection' excuse."

Holly was quiet for a moment, then said, "What if I don't fit?

I'm not fully shifter like the reindeer kids, and I'm not fully human like the human students. I'm just... between."

Connor's heart squeezed. He'd known this conversation was coming, had lived it himself in different ways. "Between isn't bad, Holly. Between is where the most important work happens."

"That's easy to say when you built a whole school around being between," Holly muttered.

"It wasn't easy," Connor said quietly. "Your mom and I were terrified. We thought we'd fail, that we weren't enough, that being between made us weaker instead of stronger." He took her hand. "But being between meant we could see both worlds clearly. We could build bridges because we stood on both sides."

"What if I can't build bridges? What if I just fall through the gap?"

"Then we catch you." Kayla appeared in the doorway, crossing to sit on Holly's other side. "That's what family does. That's what this academy does. We catch the ones who fall and help them find their footing."

Holly leaned against her mother. "Were you scared? When you started at North Pole University?"

"Terrified," Kayla admitted. "Every single day. I was the only human in most of my classes. I didn't know if I belonged, if I was strong enough, if anyone would accept me." She brushed Holly's hair back. "But I learned that belonging isn't about fitting perfectly into one category. It's about showing up as yourself and trusting that's enough."

"And it was," Connor added. "Your mom became the first human Oath Keeper. She proved that magic isn't about blood, it's about will and heart."

Holly was quiet, processing. Then: "You really think I can do this? Start at the academy and not embarrass you?"

"I think you're going to be exactly who you need to be,"

Connor said. "And if anyone has a problem with that, they'll answer to me."

"And me," Kayla added fiercely.

Holly smiled, small but genuine. "Okay. I'll try."

Later, after both kids were asleep, Connor and Kayla stood on their small balcony watching the aurora dance overhead. At thirty-five, they'd grown into their roles, Connor as Headmaster, Kayla as Director of Human-Creature Relations, in ways they never could have imagined that morning they'd planted a tree in an empty field.

"She's scared," Kayla said quietly, leaning into Connor's embrace.

"She's brave," Connor corrected. "Being scared and doing it anyway, that's the definition of courage."

Through their bond, twelve years strong and still as present as the day it formed, he felt Kayla's agreement mixed with her own lingering worry.

"We did the right thing, didn't we?" she asked. "Building the academy. Raising our kids here. Asking them to be pioneers just like we were."

Connor turned her to face him. "We built something that matters. A place where kids like Holly and Cole don't have to choose between worlds because both worlds exist in the same space. Where being between isn't a weakness, it's an identity worth celebrating."

"But it's hard for them."

"It was hard for us too," Connor reminded her. "And we survived. We thrived. We built this." He gestured to the campus spread before them, lights glowing in windows, the sound of student laughter drifting on the wind, the tree they'd planted now tall and strong in the courtyard.

Kayla rested her head on his shoulder. "Do you ever wonder

what would have happened if we'd said no? If we'd taken different jobs, lived somewhere else, let someone else build this dream?"

"Never," Connor said firmly. "This was always meant to be ours. We were always meant to build it together."

The aurora blazed brighter overhead, ribbons of green and gold weaving patterns that seemed almost deliberate, as if the land itself was affirming his words.

"Twelve years ago, we planted a tree and promised to build something worth inheriting," Kayla murmured. "I think we kept that promise."

"We're still keeping it," Connor said. "Every day. Every student who walks through those doors. Every kid who learns they don't have to choose between parts of themselves. Every bridge we help them build."

Inside, their children slept, Holly with her books still spread across her bed, Cole with his stuffed reindeer clutched tight. Half-human, half-shifter, wholly themselves. Living proof that the academy worked, that integration wasn't just possible but natural, that the future could be kinder than the past.

The northern pine swayed in the night wind, its branches casting shadows across the courtyard where tomorrow, students would gather and learn and grow.

"Ready for another year?" Kayla asked.

Connor pulled her closer. "Ready for a lifetime."

They stood together in comfortable silence, watching their academy breathe with life, the impossible dream made real.

The bond marks on their wrists caught the aurora light, glowing faintly. Twelve years faded but still visible, still proof of what they'd chosen.

Tomorrow, Holly would face her fears. Cole would practice his shifts. Connor and Kayla would return to their offices and tackle the thousand small decisions that kept an academy running.

But tonight was for this, for standing together under the northern lights, for feeling the bond hum between them, for knowing that whatever came next, they'd face it as they'd faced everything else.

The End.

Did you enjoy *Wedded Bliss*?

Please consider leaving a review on Goodreads, Bookbub or your favorite retailer. Reviews help me reach new readers.

This concludes the **North Pole University** series. Read all about Holly's adventure at **North Pole Academy** in **Mistletoe Misfits**.

Have you read **Oath Keeper**?

This FREE North Pole University story is set between **Holiday Shifters** and **Freshman Frost**

ABOUT THE AUTHOR

Positive, uplifting books and stories.

Marie-Hélène Lebeault is the author of *The Evers Series, Clarity Castle, What Happens Next? Readers Decide Which Story Becomes a Book, the Blood Magick Trilogy, Holiday Shifters, Ghost Stories, Defenders of the Realm, Utopia, Chronicles of the Starborne Cadets, Legends Reborn,* as well as a series of picture books called Fairy Grandmother. She lives in Canada with her grown children.

www.mhlebeault.com

Follow on Social Media, she'd love to hear from you!

facebook.com/mhlebeaultauthor
x.com/mhlebeault
instagram.com/mhlebeault
amazon.com/author/mhlebeault
bookbub.com/authors/marie-helene-lebeault
goodreads.com/mhlebeault
linkedin.com/in/mhlebeault
tiktok.com/@mhlebeaultauthor

ALSO BY THE AUTHOR

North Pole University - NA Paranormal Romance

Holiday Shifters

Freshman Frost

Sophomore Solstice

Junior Jinx

Senior Spark

Wedded Bliss

Mistletoe Misfits

Legends Reborn - NA Fairytale Retellings

A Curse of Snow and Ash

A Curse of Thorns and Slumber

A Curse of Glass and Shadows

A Curse of Scars and Silver

The Chronicles of the Starborne Cadets - YA Space Opera

Confluence of Destinies (Prequel)

Stars Beyond Realms

Shadows of Orion

Echoes of the Void

The Nebula's Heart

The Starborne Paradox

Defenders of the Realm - YA Epic Fantasy

A Journey to Power

The Quest for the Emerald Rattleback

A Summer of Discovery

The Quest for the Sacred Tree

A Summer of Opposites

The Quest for the Phantom Feather

A Summer of Courage

The Quest for the Kraken's Ink

A Summer of Destiny

The Quest for the Cursed Mirrors

A Summer of Unity

Defenders of the Realm - Special Edition Hardcover Set

The Evers Series - YA Science Fantasy

The Ancestors' Key

The Academy

The Time Walker

The World Jumper

5th Anniversary Edition Omnibus

The Traveler's Handbook

The Lost Key

Blood Magick Trilogy - YA Urban Fantasy

The Blood Mage

Blood Magick

Blood Legacy

Extended Edition Omnibus

Standalones

Clarity Castle

What Happens Next?

Ghost Stories

Echoes of Tomorrow

Utopia

Picture Books

Fairy Grandmother: Millie Goes to Antarctica

Fairy Grandmother: Millie Goes to the North Pole

Fairy Grandmother: Millie Goes to China

Fairy Grandmother: Millie Goes to Africa

(Also available in French, Spanish, German, and Italian)

www.ingramcontent.com/pod-product-compliance
Lightning Source LLC
Chambersburg PA
CBHW030537180626
46810CB00005B/1909